Hand-
lettered
by the
author

PUBLISHED BY BLOOMSBURY
PUBLISHING, NEW YORK, LONDON & BERLIN
DISTRIBUTED TO THE TRADE
BY HOLTZBRINCK PUBLISHERS

LIBRARY OF CONGRESS
CATALOGING-IN-PUBLICATION DATA
AVAILABLE ON REQUEST
LCCN: 2005040987

ISBN-10:
1-58234-672-0
ISBN-13:
978-1-58234-672-4

FIRST U.S. EDITION 2005
PRINTED IN CHINA
1 3 5 7 9 10 8 6 4 2

BLOOMSBURY PUBLISHING
CHILDREN'S BOOKS U.S.A.
175 FIFTH AVE
NEW YORK
NY 10010

the hair scare

Jeffrey Fisher

BLOOMSBURY
CHILDREN'S
BOOKS

Radbert liked
to cut,
and he liked
to cut
hair.

His mother, who had particularly attractive hair, fell asleep one afternoon.

Next in line was Father.

He was amazed and thought
Radbert was brilliant.
What would the
neighbors think?

They wanted haircuts
of their own.

Radbert cut
and cut

and cut

and cut.

Almost immediately, there was a
knock at the door; it was the King.
He wished the royal hair be cut
and he wished it be cut very nicely.
"Should you fail, there will be
trouble throughout the land",
muttered the King,
wriggling in his chair.

Radbert produced the best haircut in the history of best haircuts.

The King did not look happy.
He looked from the back,
the side, the front and the top.
An unpleasant silence
descended.

"This be the **WORST** haircut there be **EVER**", he spluttered. "There be **NO MORE SCISSORS.** I command **AN END** to hairdressers."

Nasty
hair accidents,
hair sadness
and hair riots
were on
everyone's minds.

The King's hair grew so long, no one recognized him. He was soon forgotten.

"WHO IS THAT MAN?" they asked.

There was a knock at the door.
It was the King. Again.
He wished the royal hair
be cut and commanded
it be cut very nicely.

"I'm afraid I no longer cut hair. My only interest now is in flourless chocolate cake," said Radbert.

"If my hair be not cut,
I will **FORBID** ovens,
sugar and all cocoa
products," yelled the
King. "And eggs..."

Radbert produced a better haircut than the best haircut in the history of better haircuts.

The King looked at his haircut. The haircut looked at the King.

In a great flutter
the King was lifted from
the floor

and flown directly
out of the window into
the night sky.

From then on,
the land returned
to Radbert's haircuts,
chocolate cake
and happiness.

And every now and then, the distant
grumbles of the King could be heard..........